God
is My Superhero

A.K. Kronicles

ISBN 978-1-0980-1035-5 (paperback)
ISBN 978-1-64191-698-1 (hardcover)
ISBN 978-1-64191-699-8 (digital)

Christian Faith Publishing, Inc.
832 Park Avenue
Meadville, PA 16335
www.christianfaithpublishing.com

Printed in the United States of America

For……

My brother Robert and my nephew Ruben who consistently keep me grounded in my faith by leading by example.

My friend and attorney Jonathan Stanwood who always encourages me to take the higher road instead of the lower one.

All the children in the world who would like to bring their God to school with them.

Bobby woke up with a great BIG smile on his face. It was April 28, NATIONAL SUPERHERO DAY! This was the day he could bring his most favorite superhero to school with him.

Bobby looked around his room at all his superheroes. There was Dan the Builder Man, Super Strength Man, Air Space Man, and Secret Ninja Man. All the superhero toys in Bobby's room had forceful strength and could do almost anything.

4

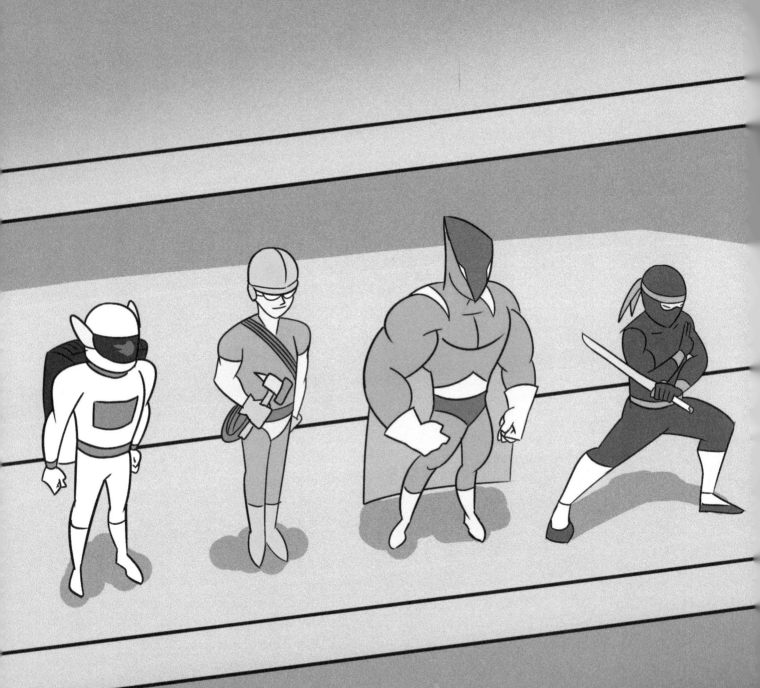

But one of Bobby's superheroes was more powerful than any of the ones in his room.

The most powerful superhero of all was much too big to fit into his room, or even his house, and it was the one he decided to bring to school with him.

8

When Bobby got to school, his teacher noticed that he was the only one in class without a superhero toy. She asked him, "Bobby, didn't you remember it was Superhero Day today?"

"Yes, I did," Bobby replied. "I have my superhero with me."

"Where is it?" Bobby's teacher said. "I don't see it anywhere."

Bobby said, "Oh, He is here. He is always with me EVERYWHERE I go. But He is much too big to ONLY fit into this classroom."

Bobby's teacher smiled and said, "Oh, I see now. He is invisible, right?"

"Sometimes," Bobby said, and then he sat down at his desk.

12

All the children in his class got up one by one from their desks to tell everyone about their superhero.

Tamika's favorite superhero was Samantha the Super Scientist because she could figure out how to make anything. She was very smart and very talented.

Danny's favorite superhero was Meteorite Man because he was faster than anyone. He could also fly straight up to the moon.

16

John's favorite superhero was the Praying Mantis because he could hypnotize criminals and put them in jail.

Sally's favorite superhero was Leprechaun Woman because she was green and always found a pot of gold.

When it was Bobby's turn, he walked up to the front of the class. As he walked past Tamika's desk, Tamika whispered to Bobby, "Where is your superhero?"

Bobby looked at Tamika and answered, "My superhero is right beside me."

"Huh? I don't see anyone," Tamika said.

Then Bobby stood in front of his class and said, "My superhero is GOD! He is so powerful He can be everywhere at the same time. He can be inside a house or up in the sky.

He can be in your classroom at school or down in the ocean where the fish live.

No matter where I am, He watches over ME! He created everything in Heaven and on Earth. And to me, He is the GREATEST SUPERHERO OF ALL."

28

The rest of the kids in the class shouted, "Can he be my SUPERHERO too?"

Bobby said, "All you have to do is BELIEVE in Him, and He can be your superhero too."

All the kids in the class shouted, "YAY!"

The End.

CPSIA information can be obtained
at www.ICGtesting.com
Printed in the USA
LVHW072026271222
735837LV00008B/157